A Tall Tale about a Dachshund

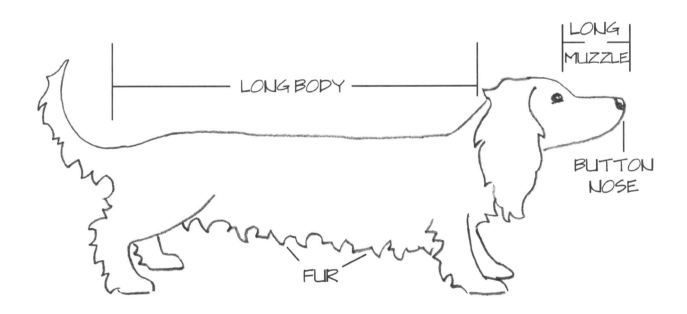

LONG MUZZLE

LONG BODY

BUTTON NOSE

FUR

Written by **Kizzie Jones**

TALL TALES

and a Pelican

How a friendship came to be

├ HARD, BONY BEAK ┤

TWO WINGS

FEATHERS

Illustrated by **Scott Ward**

This book is dedicated to the Interfaith Amigos: Pastor Don Mackenzie, Rabbi Ted Falcon & Sheikh Jamal Rahman in appreciation for modeling that we can like one another without being alike. We just need to get to know each other. — KJ

Dedicated to Cameron, my person-friend, and Dexter, my Schnauzer-friend. — SW

Author Kizzie Jones contact:
www.kizziejones.com

Illustrator Scott Ward contact:
www.scottwardart.com

Designed by Nelson Agustín
Publishing consultation by Brian Schwartz
Edited by EPIC the Edmonds Writing Community & the Writing Sisters

ISBN: 978-0-9973641-0-1

A Tall Tale about a Dachshund and a Pelican

Once upon a time, long, long ago,
a little girl and her dachshunds
lived by a magical sea.
They loved to romp on the soft sand.

One day, Goldie, one of her dachshunds, saw the most amazing creature.

It had a long muzzle like hers.
It had a long body like hers.

Goldie thought,
"I could really like someone who
looks so much like me."

9

Curious, Goldie crept closer.

The creature spoke,
"Hello, are you lost?"

"Oh no," said Goldie.
"I came to meet you.
We look so much alike.
I thought we might be friends."

The creature gasped.
"Alike? You think we look alike?"

Goldie said,
"Yes! Look,
we both have
long muzzles
and long bodies."

11

"Wait and watch,"
the creature said
and opened its massive mouth.

It did not look
anything like Goldie's.
The creature had a hard
and bony beak, no nose,
and a deep stretchy pouch
filled with fish.

Goldie's muzzle had
soft golden fur on top,

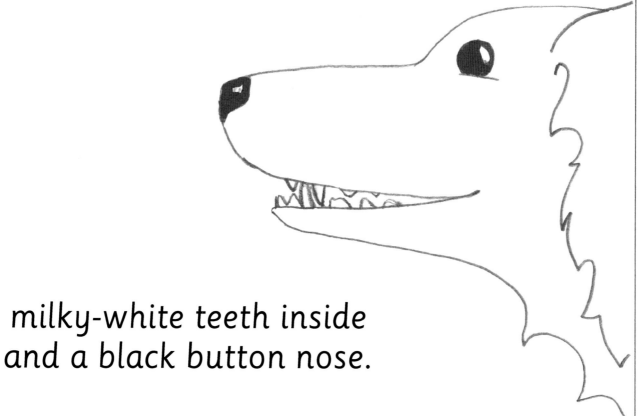

milky-white teeth inside
and a black button nose.

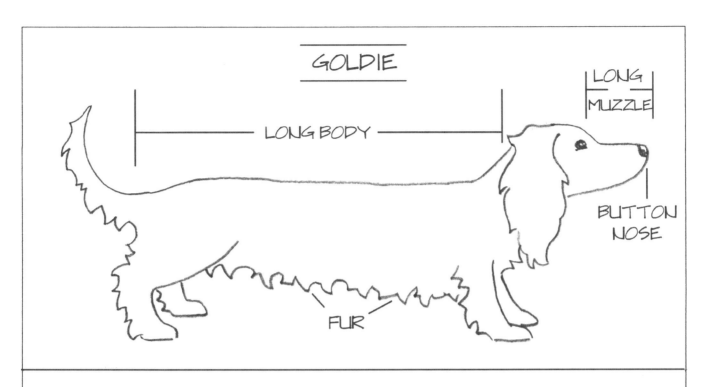

Goldie, a determined dachshund,
tried again.

She said,
"Well, at least we both have long bodies."

14

HARD, BONY BEAK

THE CREATURE

TWO WINGS

FEATHERS

"Yes, long bodies,
but yours is covered in golden fur.
Mine is covered in brown feathers.
Besides, I have two wings to help me fly,"
said the creature.

"Fly?"echoed Goldie.

The creature
took a few steps,
flapped its wings,

and soared over
the soft sand!

17

Goldie thought
if she tried hard enough
she could follow
the creature up
into the air.

She ran fast.
Her long furry ears
flapped and caught
the wind.

But try as she might, she could not fly.

18

The creature landed.

Goldie realized
they were
different,
very different.

19

Sadly, Goldie looked away.

"We are not the same after all," she said.

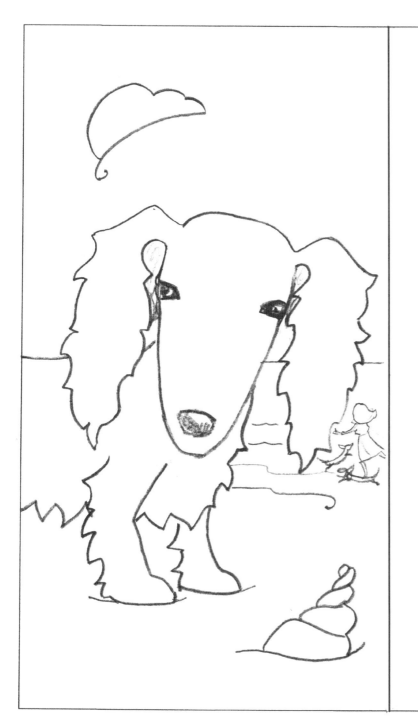

"I thought
if we were alike,
we could
be friends.

Maybe I
should go."

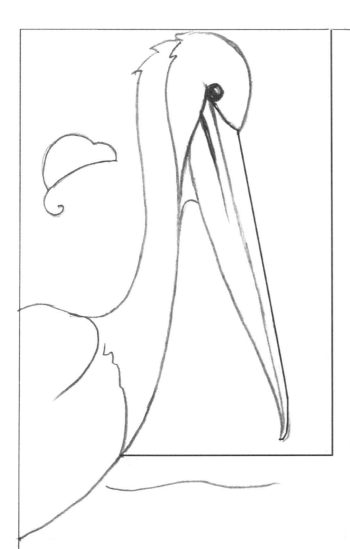

"Please stay.
We can like
each other without
being alike.
We just need to
get to know
each other better.

Let me tell you
about myself,"
the creature said.

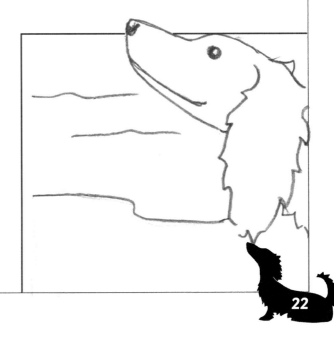

22

"I am different because I am a bird
—a pelican.
I use my huge mouth
to breathe and
scoop up fish from the sea."

"And I am a dog—a dachshund,"
said Goldie.
"I use my nose to sniff
and my strong teeth to chew."

24

Pelican said,
"The webbed skin between
    my claws helps me swim."

Goldie said, "I have nails
on my paws to help me dig.
    I use my four legs to walk
        with the little girl."

"So, you
already have
a friend who
is not like you?"
Pelican asked.

25

"Oh, I get it!" said Goldie. "Yes, the little girl and I are different, too. Yet we are very good friends. Pelican, you are right! All kinds of creatures can like each other without being alike."

That day the dachshund
and the pelican shared
the first of many
fun times together.

And that is how a friendship between
a dachshund and a pelican came to be.

The end.

About the Author

Kizzie Jones blends her love of dachshunds and her love of the ocean to create this whimsical tall tale to delight readers of all ages. Kizzie has been published in *Northwest Primetime, Chaplaincy Today, military. com*, and has been a first place non-fiction winner for Writers on the Sound.

A Tall Tale About a Dachshund and a Pelican is a sequel to *How Dachshunds Came To Be.* Mini long-haired Josie in Kizzie's arms is the story's featured dachshund, Goldie. Kizzie and her ultimate hero, Thom, with their three dachshunds— Josie, Buster and Lacey—live happily ever after in the seaside town of Edmonds, Washington.

kizziejones.com

About the Illustrator

Scott Ward creates images reflecting the vitality of the human spirit while pushing the limits of the imagination. He has worked in advertising, clothing, graphics, interiors, theater, landscapes, and murals.

Scott has always loved drawing, painting, and creating. How fun is that? Scott lives in Seattle.

scottwardart.com

29

Praise for How **DACHSHUNDS** Came To Be

"A must-have for a primary school or public library... perfect for initiating meaningful discussions and exploring 'what if' questions."
— *Marianne Stewart, Retired Early Childhood Educator*

"Kizzie's tall tale is as much fun as low tide at the beach!... she weaves in the practice of leaving living creatures in their natural habitat... Kizzie gives voice to sea creatures rarely heard from... Scott's charming illustrations... help imaginations of all ages run wild with the dachshunds on the sand!"
— *Laura Firth Markley, Beach Naturalist and Researcher*

"...Young children will be mesmerized by the sophisticated yet accessible language and metaphors. ...art work is gorgeous...warm-hearted story that will be a joy to read over and over!
— *Kim Votry, Author,* My Own Magic

"Brimming with the kindness of friends... a magical seaside tale!"
— *Mary Kay Sneeringer, Owner Edmonds Bookshop*

"...this whimsical touching fable models the values of compassion, collaboration, and love as caring pathways for creating understanding and empathy for others.
—*Ellin Snow, MSW*

30

To purchase How Dachshunds Came To Be, please visit **kizziejones.com**

Made in the USA
Middletown, DE
14 April 2022